More from the Molesons

More from the
Molesons

Stories by Burny Bos
Pictures by Hans de Beer

Translated by J. Alison James

North-South Books
New York / London

Copyright © 1995 by Nord-Süd Verlag AG, Gossau Zürich, Switzerland
First published in Switzerland under the title *Familie Maulwurf, Alles im Griff!*
English translation copyright © 1995 by North-South Books Inc.

First published in the United States, Great Britain, Canada,
Australia, and New Zealand in 1995 by North-South Books,
an imprint of Nord-Süd Verlag AG, Gossau Zürich, Switzerland.

Distributed in the United States by North-South Books Inc., New York.

Library of Congress Cataloging-in-Publication Data is available.
ISBN 1-55858-407-2 (TRADE BINDING)
ISBN 1-55858-408-0 (LIBRARY BINDING)

A CIP catalogue record for this book
is available from The British Library.

1 3 5 7 9 TB 10 8 6 4 2
1 3 5 7 9 LB 10 8 6 4 2
Printed in Belgium

Contents

She zipped her chair into reverse and roared backwards.

Too bad Grandma doesn't have eyes in the back of her head, like Mother. With a *Zzippp*-KAPOW! she ran right into the ladder.

Now get this: In slow motion the ladder crumples over. Father flips backwards and lands in Grandma's lap. The paint can spins in the air, a fountain of blue. It was one of those moments you never forget.

All the commotion woke up Mother. She took us to the park to play while Grandma went home to clean up.

What Grandma didn't know was that Dusty and I had slipped the sign on the back of her chair: CAUTION! WET PAINT!"

Family Bunk Bed

One morning we woke up to the sound of pounding. I jumped out of bed and went to see what was happening.

Father was outside with a pile of wood and nails and glue. He was busily making something.

"What is it?" I asked.

"Ghrumph," he said through the nails in his mouth.

He was hard at work all day long. Dusty and I hung around trying to find out what he was doing, but all he would say was "Wait and see."

Mother Knows Best

One day it was so windy, the trees bent in half. Father looked outside.

"Now, *this* is a day to fly a kite," he said.

"Isn't it too windy?" asked Mother.

"It's perfect," Father said. "I hate it when there is just a little puff of wind— the kite never gets off the ground. Come on, Dug and Dusty."

A minute later we were all out in the field with our kite.

At first I tried to hold the kite while
Father let out the string, but the wind
ripped it right out of my hands. Dusty
took the other side.

Father started to run. "Let go!" he
shouted.

The kite shot like an arrow into the sky.
Father had to brace himself against the
wind, the kite pulled so strongly.

I wanted to try to fly the kite. "It's my
turn," I shouted, pulling on Father's arm.

"I don't think so," said Father.

"I don't think so," said Dusty.

"You're both crazy," I said.

"The wind is much too strong," Father said. "I can barely hold it myself. I'm going to try to bring it down."

But the kite was having a great time up there in the strong wind. Father groaned and grunted and tugged at the line. A tree branch cracked and fell to the ground.

"You two go on inside," said Father. "I'll get the kite down in one piece."

"Okay," said Dusty. "We might as well."

"Since we're not even allowed to fly the
kite ourselves," I said.

Father was out for another hour. When
he came into the house, he fell like a
stone on the sofa.

"Watch this!" cried Father. "I'm going to do a jump." He skated fast, did a quick turn, and—

"*Look out!*" I shouted. Father was headed right for Dusty's chair. I ducked, and Father flew over Dusty and landed with a cracking thud on the ice.

That must have hurt, I thought.

But the cracking sound didn't stop. It wasn't Father. The ice had sprung a leak.

"Wow, that was great," Dusty said.

Father scrambled to his feet and skated around the edge of the pond one more time, as if nothing was wrong. But then suddenly he wanted to go home.

We didn't mind at all.

The Market Crash

Usually Father goes shopping for the weekend, but this Friday he was painting the kitchen. So Mother took Dusty and me along to help.

"I'm in a good mood," said Mother. "Let's get something for a treat."

"I want popcorn!" cried Dusty.

I wanted a giant bar of chocolate.

Before long, we had a whole load of groceries. There was a long wait at the check-out.

Finally it was our turn. The lady at the check-out scanned in the prices. The machine whirred and pinged. "That will be sixty-eight forty-seven," said the lady.

Mother stared into her purse, shocked.